Elaine L. Anderson

This book is dedicated to my children Ross and Eve

Elaine Anderson is an infant teacher and a practising Baptist. Her husband is a lecturer and they have two children.

Illustrated by Lee Gallaher

First published 1990
Second printing 1991

Printed and published by The Stanborough Press Limited
for Autumn House Publications, Alma Park, Grantham, NG31 9SL, England.

ISBN 0-904748-63-4

One night deep in the jungle Little Mouse stirred from his sleep. His eyes were wide with excitement, and his nose twitched and searched for a scent in the air. Fear gripped him. Someone was there! Little Mouse kept perfectly still and tense, ready to move quickly should he have to.

From somewhere a gentle voice said:

"Do not be afraid, Little Mouse, I have not come to harm you. My name is Jesus, and I've come to speak to you."

Mouse looked up into a caring, smiling face and completely lost all his fear as this lovely being picked him up and cupped him in his hands.

"Mouse, listen to what I have to say, and listen well. There is important work to be done, and I want you to help me. I am coming back soon to take home all who love me and keep my ways. I want all my creatures to know this, and to get ready. That's where I need your help, Mouse. I want you to tell all the jungle to get ready soon, so they can come home with me."

"Mmmmm . . . me?" whispered Mouse.

"Surely one as great as you, Jesus, knows that of all the animals in the jungle I am one of the smallest, and most hunted. I live every day in fear of death — how can I help you?"

"Of all the animals in the jungle, Mouse, I have chosen you to do my work. You needn't be afraid, I am with you always and I will protect you. The most important thing is, do you really want to help me?"

Mouse looked up into the dark, caring eyes, and felt the warmth of the rough hands which lovingly held him.

"Oh, yes, I will help you", said Mouse.

"Then tomorrow start your work. Tell everyone what they must do. Don't worry about what to say, Little Mouse, I will give you the words."

Jesus bent down and gently laid Mouse on the ground.

"Go now, and sleep well. Tomorrow you have great things to do. Remember, I am with you always, even when you can't see me."

Mouse watched and blinked his eyes as Jesus walked away. He shuffled back to his nest and settled down to sleep, thinking of all the work he had to do in the morning.

At the crack of dawn Mouse got up and started at once to visit all the animals one by one. He followed the river, and the first animal he called on was Alligator.

"Alligator!" Mouse called out in his strongest voice.

"Alligator, it's me, Mouse. I have something important to tell you."

Alligator popped up out of the river and his eyes rested on the water's surface like two bubbles.

"Yes?" gurgled Alligator. "What is it?"

"Lord Jesus came to see me last night, Alligator, and he told me to tell everyone to get ready, because he's coming back soon."

Alligator listened and thought a moment.

"When?" he asked. "What day is he coming?"

"I don't know the exact day," said Mouse, "but we must start to get ready now."

"Mmmmm, to be honest, I'm a bit tied up at the moment. I've such a lot on — I could let you see my diary — it's completely full. I'm going to my sister's this Friday, the dentist on Saturday, and . . . let's see now."

Alligator snapped his mouth open and shut, and clicked his teeth together in a manner which really frightened Mouse, but he tried hard to be strong, and think of the promise that Jesus had made to protect him.

"I could fit him in a week on Thursday. Would that be any good? Otherwise I'm afraid I'm busy till the end of June."

"It's very important", said Mouse. "He's coming to take home all the creatures who love him and keep his ways."

"Mmmmm", said Alligator again. "Well, if it's a week on Thursday tell him I'll come." And with that Alligator floated off.

The next animal that Mouse met along the river was Hippopotamus.

"Hippopotamus", said Mouse. "I must talk to you!"

Hippopotamus plopped out of the muddy river-bank, yawned, and said:

"Y-e-s, Mouse?" in a long drawl.

"Hippopotamus, Lord Jesus came to see me last night, and he told me to tell everyone to get ready, because he's coming back soon."

"Oh, is he?" said Hippopotamus, yawning again. "That's nice."

"Yes", said Mouse. "We've got to get ready, because when he comes he's going to take home all the creatures who love him and keep his ways."

"Right!" said Hippopotamus. "I'll do it. I'll get ready. Tomorrow."

"NO!" said Mouse as firmly as he could. "There's no time to waste. We must start to tell everyone today!"

"Look, I said I'd do it, didn't I? But not today. I can't just drop everything at a moment's notice and trek all over the jungle with you. I've got things to do. Come round tomorrow, or better still, the day after, and I'll be ready then."

With that, Hippopotamus waddled off, yawning again.

Mouse was becoming a bit unhappy but he remembered what Jesus had said, and he kept on going. While Mouse was walking he met Puma, who was in the middle of his daily exercises. Puma was lying on the ground, doing press-ups.

"145, 146, 147", he counted, puffing.

"Puma", said Mouse.

"Hi!" puffed Puma. "148, 149, 150."

"Puma, could we talk for a minute? I have something important to tell you."

"Sure", said Puma,
laying down and rubbing his head with a towel.

"Lord Jesus came to see me last night, Puma, and he told me to tell everyone to get ready because he's coming back soon."

"Do you do any exercises, Mouse? You could do with some. Just look at your sagging tummy, and that tail of yours, well! I've got just the book for you."

"*First Steps in Fitness* it's called. You'll like it."

"I don't want your book, Puma", said Mouse. "I'm far too busy. I've got to tell all the Jungle about Jesus. Please, Puma, won't you listen?"

"My friend Pat borrowed it you know, and within a week his muscles were bulging. His own mother walked past him! Imagine!"

Mouse sadly shook his head and walked off. It was no use, it was as if Puma couldn't even hear him. He felt more sad than ever, and wondered if Jesus really knew what he was doing giving him, Little Mouse, the job of telling the Jungle. He shuffled on, but grew tired, so he rested at the bottom of a tree.

"What'sss the matter with you?" hissed Snake, and Mouse almost jumped out of his skin.

"Oh, hello!" said Mouse, trying to look happy. "It's nice to see you!"

"You look awful", snapped Snake.

"Er . . . well, I am a bit tired, but really, I feel fine. Snake, I'm glad to meet you, because Lord Jesus came to see me last night, and he told me to tell all the Jungle to get ready because he's coming back soon."

"What doesss he mean — get ready? Why doesn't he get the Jungle ready, it'sss hisss Jungle, isn't it? Why doesn't he tidy it up, if he'sss so good, eh? What doesss he do all day, anyway?"

Snake slithered nearer to Mouse as he hissed:

"Last week two tigersss mugged my cousin Ida, and left her for dead. What'sss right about that, eh? If he caresss why didn't he send a thunderbolt to kill those tigersss?"

Snake was lying on his tummy and looking Mouse fairly and squarely in the face, his blue eyes blazing.

Mouse cleared his throat and said:

"It's not his fault, Snake. He didn't hurt your cousin Ida. He loves us all. Please help to tell everyone to get ready. We haven't much time."

"No!" snapped Snake. "Tell him I'll only come if he killsss the two tigersss that got Ida."

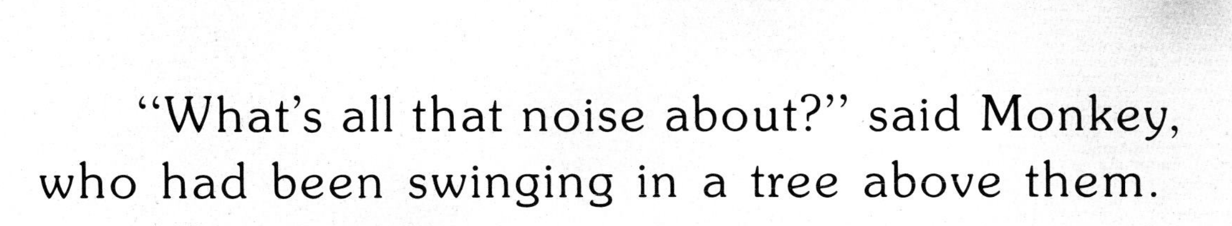

"What's all that noise about?" said Monkey, who had been swinging in a tree above them.

Mouse cleared his throat once more, and told Monkey all about Jesus coming, and told him to get ready.

"How do you know that it was really him?" asked Monkey.

"Did you ask to see his I.D. card?"

"No," said Mouse, "but I know it was him."

"It probably wasn't then. I don't want to sound cheeky, Mouse, but would the real Jesus ask a mouse to tell the Jungle? Would he? The real Jesus would ask Lion, or Elephant or perhaps even me, but not a mouse! It's not likely! Really, Mouse, you believe anything! You've been tricked."

Mouse wearily went home and thought about his day's work. He felt like giving up, but then he remembered Jesus' comforting words:

"Don't be afraid.
I am always with you."

The next day Mouse decided to see the King of the Jungle himself, and went at once to Lion's den. Lion was lying on his back while a monkey fanned him with a large leaf.

"Lion", said Mouse. "May I talk to you?"

"Of course", said Lion. "How can I help you?"

"Well, I may be able to help you", said Mouse. "Lord Jesus came to see me, and he asked me to tell all the Jungle to get ready because he's coming back soon."

All at once there was a deafening roar, and Mouse stood rooted to the spot with fear. Then he saw that Lion wasn't angry, he was roaring with laughter!

"Mouse, you are so amusing! When Jesus told you to tell all the Jungle he didn't mean me! I don't need to get ready. I'm the King of the Jungle. It's obvious Jesus will take me first, before you all. Ha! Ha! Ha! . . . "

Lion burst into another fit of loud laughter, and wiping a tear from his eye with a large furry paw, he went on:

"It's very kind of you to tell me, Mouse, but Jesus will probably get in touch with me personally to fix up the departure details. When he does, I'll pass them on to you. Run along now, there's a good chap."

Mouse felt sure that Lion had really got it all wrong, but before he could say so, he was pushed outside and sent on his way.

Mouse decided to go and see Elephant, who was standing knee-deep in the river, giving himself a shower.

"Elephant!" shouted Mouse from the river-bank. "I really want to talk to you. Can you come to the water's edge?"

"Sure", spluttered Elephant, and plodded over. "What do you want?"

"Jesus has been to see me, Elephant, and he says we've all to get ready. He's coming back soon, and he's taking home all the creatures who love him and keep his ways."

"Oh", said Elephant, thinking very deeply and twitching his large ears.

"Mouse, did he say anything about me, at all, when he spoke to you?" asked Elephant.

"No", said Mouse. "He only told me to tell everyone to get ready."

"Ah", said Elephant, and thought again for a while.

"It's terribly worrying, Mouse", said Elephant. "Oh, I do hope he saw me the day I carried six monkeys on my back so they could cross the river, and then there was the time when Antelope had a fever and I gave her cold showers to bring her temperature down, and then . . . ."

"Oh, I'm sure he saw you", interrupted Mouse.

"But will he remember all my good deeds? I'm not the only elephant in the Jungle, you know. What if I've been doing all these good deeds to get to Heaven and another elephant goes in my place? Elephants never forget, but does Jesus?"

Elephant twitched his ears again and looked at the sky.

"It's so very worrying", he muttered.

"Don't worry, Elephant, Jesus never forgets", said Mouse. "But we must make sure all the other animals know about Jesus. Will you come with me?"

"No, I won't come with you, Mouse", said Elephant. "I'd better stay here and do some more good deeds, until he comes. Perhaps I should write them down this time, just in case he does forget. Thanks for tipping me off about Jesus, though."

Just then Elephant saw the fat Rhinoceros struggling to get out of the water, and before Mouse could say any more to him, Elephant went thundering along shouting:

"Stay there! I'll help you! Wait for me to pull you out!" And he disappeared.

Mouse felt sad when he saw Elephant running away, because he had really wanted to tell Elephant more about Jesus.

Mouse spent many days and many weeks telling all the animals, but no one came with him, and no one helped him. One night he flopped into his nest, tired, hungry and very sad. His poor feet were red and sore with walking, and his eyes stung because they were so tired.

"I've let you down, Jesus." He whispered into the darkness, his voice close to tears. "Nobody listened. It's all gone wrong."

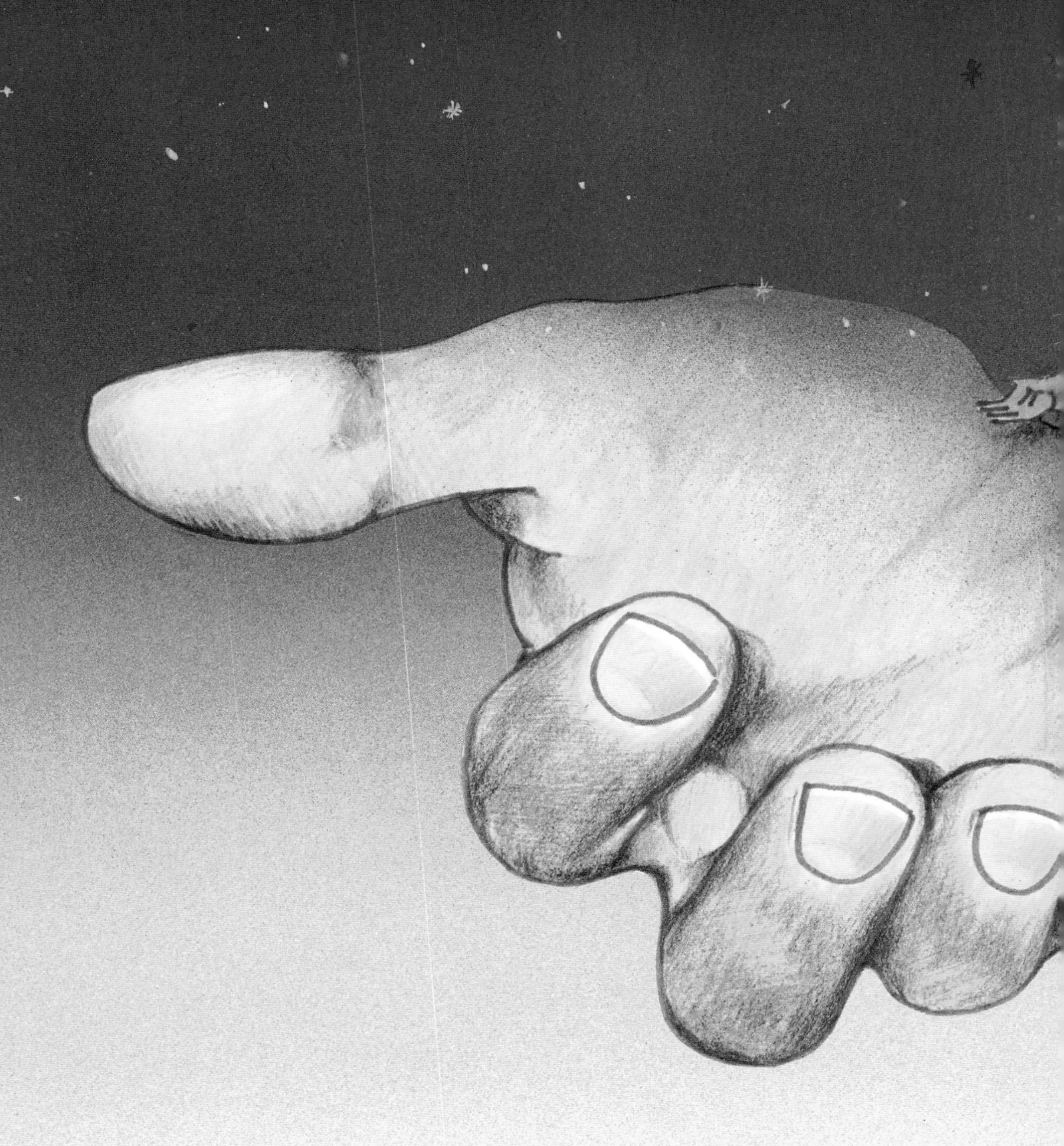

Mouse closed his eyes and fell asleep almost at once. Far into the night, when all the Jungle was asleep, Mouse awoke, feeling strangely restless. Then he heard a familiar voice say:

"It's me, Mouse. I've come to take you home."

Mouse blinked his eyes, and looked again into the lovely face of Jesus.

"Jesus," sniffed Mouse, "nobody listened. I've

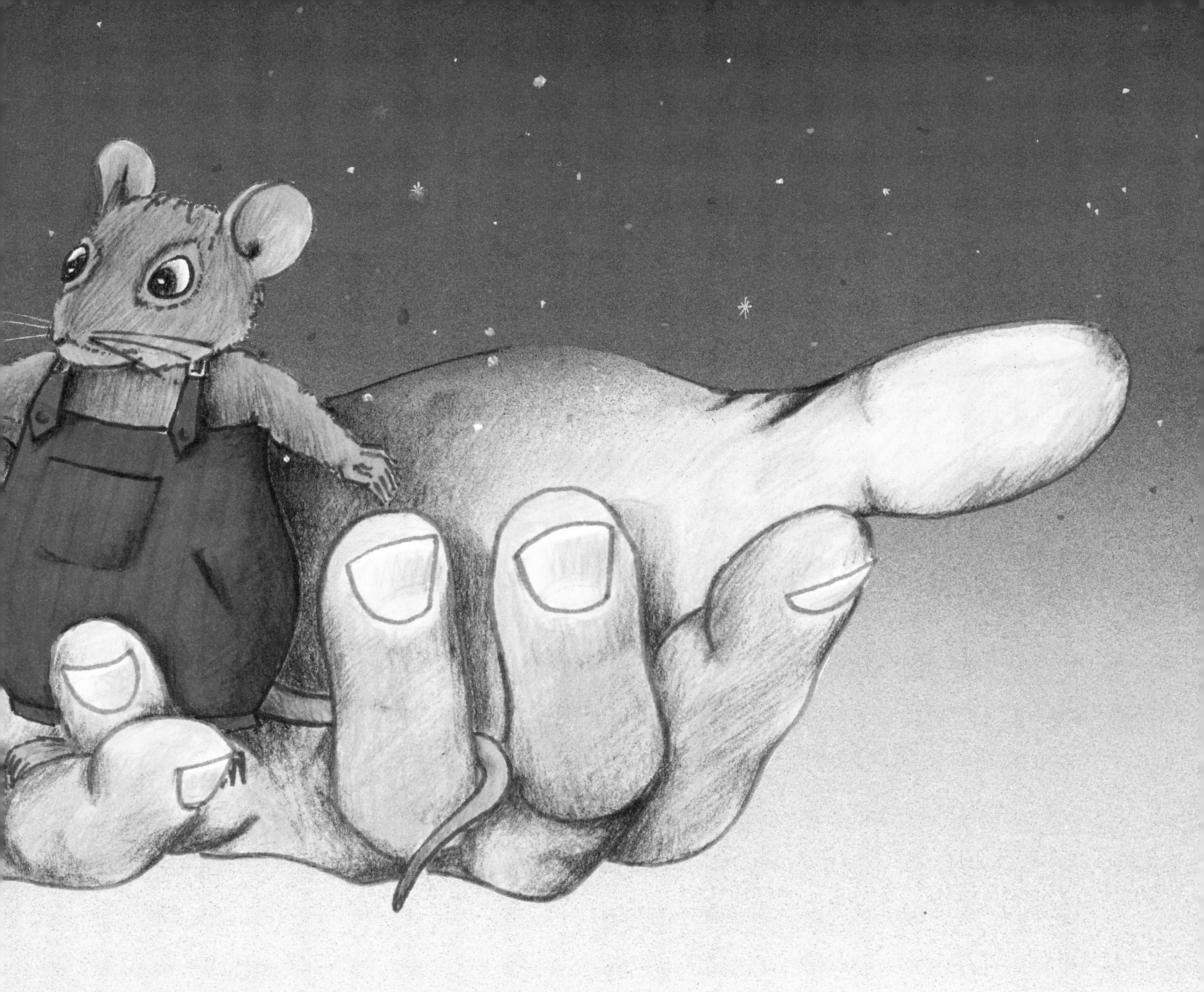

ruined it for you. Oh, I'm sorry . . ." Mouse started to cry.

"Dry your tears, Mouse. You did as I asked, and I am proud of you. Out of all the Jungle I have chosen to take you home with me. And you are not alone. Hippopotamus got ready after all . . . .'

Jesus cupped Mouse in his hands, and Mouse felt so happy he thought his heart would burst.

MOUSE'S SONG

Words and music by Fran Kittle

Deep in the jungle the very next day,
The little brown mouse was quick to obey.
He told all the animals at work and play —
Told them Jesus was on his way.
But the animals paid no heed.

Deep in the jungle not a creature stirred.
Only the prayers of the mouse were heard.
Then out of the clouds there came a voice,
"You did as I asked, oh little mouse,
So I've come to take you home."

FINAL CHORUS:

"You told all the animals one by one.
Told them I'm ready, my time is come.
Told them to hurry, but they only waved,
No time to listen, no time to be saved."